LEGO EXO-FORCE

GHOST OF THE PAST

BY GREG FARSHTEY

SCHOLASTIC IN

New York   Toronto   London   Auckland   Sydney
Mexico City   New Delhi   Hong Kong   Buenos Aires

ISBN-13: 978-0-439-92326-2

ISBN-10: 0-439-92326-3

12 11 10 9 8 7 6 5 4 3 2 1   7 8 9 10 11/0

Printed in the U.S.A.
First printing, June 2007

CHAPTER 1

Ha-Ya-To slammed his hand against the red button on his battle machine's control panel, then did it twice more. Each time, the monitor screen in the Gate Guardian's cockpit flashed the same message: "Energy Level 4%. Thruster Boost Impossible."

Great, the EXO-FORCE pilot grumbled. *A mile up, an Iron Condor on my tail, and this tin can runs out of juice!*

At least the Iron Condor's mechanical pilot was giving him some room to maneuver. At the start of the conflict between robots and humans, a Devastator robot pilot would have closed in as soon as it saw a damaged EXO-FORCE battle machine, but not anymore. Hikaru had tricked them a few too many times by pretending the

Stealth Hunter was out of power and then attacking as soon as they got close.

An Iron Condor missile whizzed by, just missing the Gate Guardian's right arm. Ha-Ya-To tried, but he couldn't think of a way out. With so little power left, his battle machine couldn't outfly the Iron Condor or outfight it. *Looks like my only option is to get blown out of the sky,* he said to himself.

Just then, something caught his eye down below. It was another EXO-FORCE battle machine rocketing up from the Golden City. As it came closer, Ha-Ya-To could see it was Hikaru piloting the Sky Guardian. Before Ha-Ya-To could even broadcast a hello, the Sky Guardian was firing missiles at the Iron Condor. Caught by surprise, the Iron Condor turned around and flew at top speed back to the robot side of Sentai Mountain.

"Are you okay?" Hikaru asked through his battle machine's communicator.

"I've got enough spark to make it down," Ha-Ya-To answered. "But if you hadn't shown up, I wouldn't be landing in one piece. Thanks."

Both pilots flew back toward the Golden City, the new EXO-FORCE base. The old headquarters, Sentai Fortress, had been badly damaged by robot attacks and the

decision was made to abandon it. Now pilots and technicians were based in this mysterious city on the mountaintop.

The Gate Guardian and the Sky Guardian landed side by side. Ryo, the EXO-FORCE team's best engineer, ran out to greet the returning pilots. "What happened?" he asked Ha-Ya-To. "You should have been able to fly rings around that robot."

"Not enough power," Ha-Ya-To answered. "I need to move fast and hit hard up there, boys, and I can't do it with yesterday's battle machine. What do we have that's got some real power?"

Ryo chuckled. "Come with me. I think I might have just what you need."

Ryo's new lab in the Golden Tower looked a lot like his old one. Piles of equipment were scattered all over, half a dozen computers were running at once, and a half-eaten sandwich sat between two laser cannons. Kicking things aside as he went, Ryo led Ha-Ya-To to the back of the room.

"I can't take all the credit for this," the engineer said. "The computer gave me the idea. I just . . . tweaked it a little."

When the EXO-FORCE team had first discovered the Golden City, they had found a massive computer. The computer told Hikaru, Takeshi, and Ryo that it contained an enormous amount of information about weapons, armor, and more. But to access the information, they would have to find several codes and enter them into the machine. So far, all three pilots had found new battle machines in the Golden City, and Ryo had learned about some new technologies from the computer. Ha-Ya-To wondered what exciting invention Ryo was about to show him.

At first sight, Ha-Ya-To wasn't impressed. The battle machine Ryo unveiled was sleek and powerful-looking, but it didn't look that innovative . . . or fast. Not wanting to hurt

the engineer's feelings, Ha-Ya-To smiled and said, "Yeah, that's . . . great. I like the armor."

"No, no, this isn't the exciting part," Ryo said. He hit a button on the wall, which opened another panel. "*This* is!"

A huge conveyor belt on the ceiling began to move. Suspended from it on chains was something beyond anything Ha-Ya-To had ever seen before. At first, it just looked like a huge mass of machinery. Then he realized what he was seeing, and his eyes went wide.

It was a massive rocket pack, with three gigantic turbojet engines. Mounted on top of and around the engines were fierce laser cannons and a missile launcher. It somehow managed to be beautiful, frightening, and awe-inspiring all at the same time.

Ryo fitted the rocket pack onto the back of the battle machine and released the chains. "You can put the pack on or take it off, whenever you need to. It's made of some kind of super-light metal. But at the same time it's really strong. It's got enough power to take you into sub-orbit, or punch through a six-foot-thick wall. You could outrace a Sonic Phantom in this or fire the cannons and take it down. Get in and try it — I'm calling it the Aero Booster."

Ha-Ya-To could hardly wait. He climbed into the cockpit of the new battle machine. Some of the controls were a little confusing at first, but he got the idea pretty quickly. He was just about to twist a dial when Ryo stopped him.

"No! That triggers the afterburners —
you'll fry the whole lab!" Ryo said. "Just . . .
don't touch anything until we get it outside.
Look, Sensei Keiken has another computer
code that needs hunting down. Why don't
you go find the code and give this machine a
trial run at the same time."

Ha-Ya-To nodded. He was more than
ready to take the Aero Booster up into the
sky and see what it could really do.

CHAPTER 2

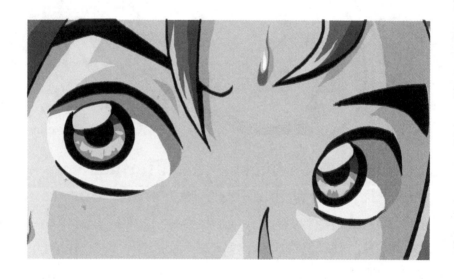

"Down there?" Ha-Ya-To asked, startled. "You want me to go down there?"

Ryo had brought him to a metallic hatch located in the rocky ground behind the Golden City. "Should be easy," the engineer said. "We open the hatch, and then you use the rocket pack engines to slow your descent into the shaft. When you reach the bottom, grab the code, and jet back up again."

Ha-Ya-To maneuvered the controls to make the Aero Booster's arm pull the hatch open. It was completely dark inside and the hole seemed to go down forever. Ryo kicked a rock into the hole and counted to himself until he heard it hit bottom. "I'd say about five and a half miles deep," Ryo said. "Maybe a little more. You better get started."

"How do we know the code is down there?"

"The computer says it is . . . and it should know," answered Ryo. "And if it was buried that deep, I'm betting it reveals something really incredible."

Ha-Ya-To nodded, trying not to look as uncomfortable as he felt. He loved to fly to any height, but he wasn't really big on being in tight places. He decided to make this the world's fastest trip underground.

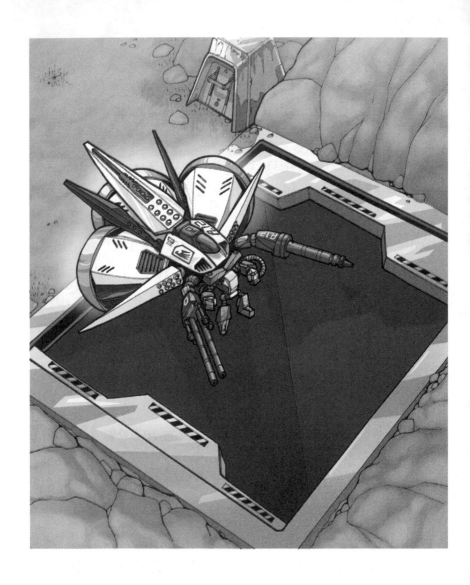

Ryo backed away as Ha-Ya-To triggered the powerful engines of the rocket pack. The Aero Booster took a step forward and dropped from sight into the hole. Ryo peered over the edge and watched the battle machine descend until it was lost from sight. Then he turned and ran back toward the Golden Tower to monitor the Aero Booster's progress.

A few moments later, a Shadow Crawler battle machine crept up onto the plateau. Spotting the open hatch, its robot pilot steered it toward the hole. One of the Shadow

Crawler's three legs reached into the shaft and secured a foothold for itself in the wall. A second leg followed and soon the Shadow Crawler was creeping silently down into the pit, stalking the Aero Booster.

By the time Ha-Ya-To reached the bottom of the shaft, he had to admit that the Aero Booster had performed well. By carefully triggering the rocket engines all the way down, he was able to slow his descent and land safely. *I hope it works just as well when it's time to get out,* he thought. *I sure wouldn't want to get stuck down here.*

Ha-Ya-To switched on the battle machine's infrared visor, which allowed him to see in the dark. There wasn't much to see, just the metal walls of the shaft and a pair of huge doors in front of him. He tried opening them using the battle machine's powerful right arm, but they stayed closed. Puzzled, he ran a quick scan.

These are blast doors, he realized. *They were made strong and thick to resist weapons or explosions and keep invaders out. Let's see how they do against my rocket pack!*

Ha-Ya-To maneuvered the Aero Booster back against the rear wall of the shaft and triggered both his laser cannons. The first shots punched deep dents in the doors, but that was all. It took another round of laser fire to finally blast them open.

Beyond the doors, it was pitch-dark and totally silent. Ha-Ya-To maneuvered the Aero Booster inside and used the battle machine's night vision to look around. He found a control box for the lab lights, but it was completely melted. He had hoped the metal plate with the code would just be sitting here, waiting for him, but there was no sign of it. Like it or not, he was going to have to go exploring.

The place looked like one of Ryo's labs. Equipment was scattered all over, some intact, some badly damaged. There were

several machines, too. Scanning them revealed something startling: They were all made of gold!

Ryo's gonna flip when he hears about this!

Ha-Ya-To activated the built-in communicator. "Aero Booster to Lab-1. Come in, Ryo," he said into the microphone. There was no answer, only static. After a few more tries, he gave up.

Too much rock between me and the city, he decided. *It's blocking the signal.*

He did another scan, this time of the entire lab. The results showed there was only this one massive chamber down here. Apparently, whoever had built the Golden City had built this place as well, and then abandoned it for some reason.

Let's hope *they remembered to turn off the stove — and the nuclear plasma generator — when they left,* Ha-Ya-To thought, as he started his search for the code.

The Shadow Crawler reached the bottom of the shaft just as Ha-Ya-To moved deeper into the lab. The Devastator robot piloting the battle machine ran its own sensor scan of the lab and the surrounding area. The pilot was not surprised by any of the results — surprise was a human reaction, after all — but one thing did make it stop and recheck its findings.

For just a moment, the scanner had shown that there were two living things inside the lab. One was the EXO-FORCE pilot, of course. But the readings from the other were like nothing the robot had ever seen before.

Whoever — or whatever — was down here with the EXO-FORCE and robot battle machines was huge, powerful . . . and most definitely not human.

CHAPTER 3

Turning back was starting to look like a really good idea to Ha-Ya-To.

The farther he went into the lab, the more unsettled he became. Some of the machines looked like the ones Ryo had in his workshop, but others seemed more like medical equipment. Notes were scattered

on tables, written in a language he didn't understand. There were also lots of diagrams of cages, force field generators, and other kinds of prison cells. Along one wall was a line of sleek, powerful-looking battle machines — all of them damaged, some practically demolished.

Wow, thought Ha-Ya-To. *I've seen battle machines dented, blasted, melted, you name it, but I've never seen anything torn apart like this. And why are they here? Were they being repaired, junked, or what? And how did they get so messed up in the first place?*

Focus on the code, he reminded himself. *Find it, bring it back, and tell Ryo all about this. Let him worry about broken battle machines and sketches of cells.*

This was easier said than done. Whoever had hidden the code had done a great job of it. The more he searched, the more strange things he found, like the pile of energy weapons near one lab table. All had been fired, some so often that the barrels were melted. But what had they been firing at?

Ha-Ya-To suddenly made the Aero Booster stop. He thought he had heard the familiar sound of metal scraping against metal. Hikaru had warned him there were robot battle machines that could hide from sensors but still made noise.

He stopped and listened. He didn't hear the sound of a battle machine in motion. No, he heard something else. It sounded like... breathing. Thinking it must be his own, he held his breath. But the sounds continued.

"Hello?" he broadcast over his battle machine intercom. "Is there someone down here?"

There was no answer. He scanned for life readings. For just a moment, one appeared on his screen, then it was gone again. It didn't match any reading he had ever seen before. *Maybe it's a glitch*, Ha-Ya-To said to himself. *Then again, maybe it's not*. He set his laser cannons to max and kept his finger near the firing button, just in case.

On the opposite side of the chamber, the Shadow Crawler stood completely still. It was hidden from the human eye by a bank of machines. A special coating on its armor made it invisible to EXO-FORCE sensors. But the robot pilot knew that any noise would give its presence away. So it watched and waited.

Its mission was simple. Thanks to a monitoring device planted on the massive computer in the Golden City, the robots learned the locations of the codes at the same time the humans did. Whenever possible, their orders were to let the humans take all the risks of finding the codes, then attack and steal them. It would wait a day, a week, or a year in the darkness of the lab in order to carry out its duty.

In the meantime, the robot would continue to watch for a repeat of that strange life reading. Regardless of whether it was an EXO-FORCE ally, anything that *lived* was an enemy of the robot army.

If Ha-Ya-To hadn't known Ryo better, he would have thought that this mission was a prank. There was definitely no code here. But Ha-Ya-To knew that Ryo's idea of humor was telling a joke like, "What did the phased anti-matter containment field say to the mass driver cannon?"

Hey, maybe this wasn't a wild goose chase after all, Ha-Ya-To said to himself. Something on one of the damaged battle machines had caught his eye. It was partially covered by shredded metal, but he was sure he saw numbers. Maneuvering the Aero Booster in that direction, he used the powerful arm of the battle machine to tear off part of the trashed battle machine. Underneath, there was a magnetic plate with a computer code engraved on it.

Got it! thought Ha-Ya-To. *Now I can get out of this hole!*

The Aero Booster's monitor screens suddenly went wild. Audio receivers had picked up the sounds of a battle machine on the move behind him. Worse, the battle machine had fired laser cannons at the Aero Booster! One blast struck his rocket pack head-on, sending Ha-Ya-To and the battle machine

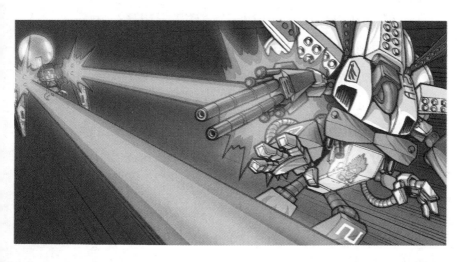

hurtling across the room. The Aero Booster crashed into the far wall.

Ha-Ya-To did an internal scan and smiled. The rocket pack had managed to survive the attack intact. That meant some robot was about to get a big surprise.

The Shadow Crawler advanced quickly toward where the Aero Booster lay in a heap. Ha-Ya-To could see its laser cannons were powering up for another shot. Fortunately, the prison pod on top of the robot battle machine was empty — no captured human pilot trapped in the pod, like there usually was.

Good, thought Ha-Ya-To. *That means I don't have to hold back. That three-legged refugee from a toaster factory is mine!*

He launched Aero Booster's missile. It never reached its target. There was a sudden blur of motion and something snatched the missile out of the air. Ha-Ya-To looked up to see a flash of wings and claws, and then both the missile and its mysterious captor were gone. A moment later, pieces of the missile came raining down, torn apart by whatever had stolen it.

What kind of robot trick was that? Ha-Ya-To thought. He ran every scan he could think of, but there was no sign of anything up near the ceiling. It was as if the winged thing had completely disappeared.

Okay, let's stay calm. Time to assess the situation. I'm five miles down with an enemy

robot and an invisible monster, Ha-Ya-To said to himself. *This situation reminds me of something my grandma used to say whenever things seemed hopeless . . .*

Uh-oh.

CHAPTER 4

Ha-Ya-To glanced at the Shadow Crawler. To his surprise, the robot battle machine was backing away, while keeping its laser cannons aimed at the ceiling. *Tinhead isn't acting like he's friends with that thing,* thought Ha-Ya-To. *Maybe I can use that to my advantage.*

"Better surrender," Ha-Ya-To said to the robot pilot, "or my pal up there might do to you what it did to that missile."

The Shadow Crawler stopped moving. The Devastator robot's head was cocked a little to one side as Ha-Ya-To's words were processed and analyzed. After a few seconds, the robot pilot said, "Your statement is incorrect. Surrender the computer code now."

Like other code plates the EXO-FORCE team had found, the one Ha-Ya-To held was magnetic. He attached it to the front of his battle machine. "Come and take it, robot. That is, unless you're worried about ol' Wings up there. You know, he comes when I call."

"Illogical. Incorrect," said the robot. "The creature prevented an attack on this unit. It therefore does not serve EXO-FORCE."

I hate it when robots are right, thought Ha-Ya-To. "So are you trying to say that big . . . whatever it is up there is working for your side?"

There was a long pause. Then the robot answered, "Negative."

One of the first things Ha-Ya-To had learned about robots was that they didn't lie. The only exception to that rule seemed to be Meca One, leader of the rebellion. But the Devastator and Iron Drone units had only two options when questioned: Tell the truth or say nothing at all.

Then another idea struck the EXO-FORCE pilot. Anything that could shred a missile could probably do the same to anything else made of metal. Was that what had happened to that row of armored battle machines? Had the chamber's mysterious resident ripped them apart?

I could live without finding that out, Ha-Ya-To thought. Takeshi would want to hunt that thing, Hikaru would want to race it, and Ryo would want to study it. Me? I'll settle for just having bad dreams about it later, when I'm safe in my bed in the Golden City.

"Let's take this fight upstairs," Ha-Ya-To said to the robot. "No point in damaging all this machinery. Hey, you might be related to some of it."

It was a day for surprises. Instead of refusing, attacking, or accusing Ha-Ya-To of planning some trick, the robot simply said, "Agreed."

The Shadow Crawler resumed backing toward the doorway. It was just about to step back into the shaft when the winged blur appeared again. Ha-Ya-To saw it swoop down toward the Shadow Crawler and strike, knocking the robot battle machine end over end. Then it shot back up toward the ceiling and vanished again.

This time, Ha-Ya-To had been fast enough to get some sensor scans. The creature was ten feet long, with a wingspan of twenty feet. Its readings didn't match anything in the Aero Booster's computer. Its claws and teeth averaged a foot long, its brain was larger than normal for a thing that size, and it had a few internal organs whose functions the minicomputer couldn't even guess at. But there was one thing the quick analysis did reveal, and that was what the flying creature ate: metal.

So our battle machines are just snacks, thought Ha-Ya-To. *But if it decides to munch on my rocket pack, I might never get out of this hole.*

The Shadow Crawler got back to its feet. A huge gash had been ripped in the side of the robot battle machine. Ha-Ya-To could see the Devastator pilot trying to broadcast a message back to its base.

"Forget it," he said. "They can't hear you."

This time, the Shadow Crawler raced at top speed for the shaft. Again, the creature shot down from above, slashed with its claws, and then soared aloft. The second attack exposed some wiring in the Shadow Crawler, which sent off a shower of sparks.

"I don't think it likes you," said Ha-Ya-To.

"Your words are illogical," said the Devastator. "Surrender the code and I will let you live."

"You'll let me —?" Ha-Ya-To repeated in disbelief. "What makes you think our friend up there is going to let you leave? It's found a new toy, robot, and it's you. Now stay out of my way — I'm getting out of here with the code."

"You cannot escape," said the Devastator.

"Just watch me!" Ha-Ya-To turned the Aero Booster's power levels up to maximum. Flames roared out of the three engines. The battle machine with Ha-Ya-To inside rocketed forward at incredible speed. Ha-Ya-To knew he would have to do a 90-degree turn straight up the shaft the second he passed through the door, or else wind up a smear on the shaft's back wall.

It turned out he had other things to worry about. Before the Aero Booster even reached the doorway, the creature had dropped down and raked its claws on the rocket pack, tearing off one of the engines. The damage threw the Aero Booster off balance. Ha-Ya-To just barely avoided crashing into a bank

of machinery. As it was, he landed very hard, hitting the stone floor and scrambling to cut off the engines before they propelled him into the wall.

When the rocket pack was safely shut down, Ha-Ya-To looked up to see the Shadow Crawler standing over him. He thought the robot battle machine might make a grab for the code, but instead the Devastator pilot just eyed him for a moment. Then it said, "I observed, as requested. When am I going to see something worthy of observation?"

"Ah, your mother was a can opener," Ha-Ya-To grumbled.

CHAPTER 5

Ha-Ya-To and the Devastator robot had been standing and staring at each other for ten minutes. Neither was willing to take his eyes off the other, for fear of an attack. Finally, Ha-Ya-To had had enough.

"This is stupid," he said.

"Explain," replied the Devastator.

"While we're having a staring contest, Wings is up on the ceiling someplace, deciding which battle machine is going to be lunch and which one dinner." Ha-Ya-To frowned. He didn't want to say what he had to say next, but there was no other choice. "Listen . . . if we are ever going to get out of here, we have to work together."

"Incorrect. Illogical," the robot answered quickly. "Robots do not work with humans.

Robots command humans. Your words do not compute."

"I'm not happy about it either," said Ha-Ya-To. "I'd like nothing better than to recycle you. But facts are facts. Alone, neither one of us can escape. Together, maybe we have a shot."

The Devastator processed the EXO-FORCE pilot's words. Destroying the human now would allow possession of the code, but the inability to escape would make it impossible to deliver the code to base. Its superiors would also require information on this hidden laboratory, which could be provided only if the Devastator escaped to deliver it. The robot calculated its options. After all, it could always destroy its enemy once they were both free.

"Agreed," said the robot. "Question: The hostile being above has attacked both our battle machines, but why not this unit or you? Analysis: It will react to us only in our battle machines. Perhaps by exiting our machines, we could reach the laboratory exit in safety."

"And then what?" asked Ha-Ya-To. "Without our battle machines, we can't get out of the shaft. We'll be stuck down here until it does notice us. No, we need data to fight this battle — I'm going to link my battle machine to one of these computers and see what I can learn. You do the same. If you find anything about that overgrown bat upstairs, sing out."

"Illogical," answered the robot. "Why would the discovery of information result in my transmitting melodic sounds?"

"Never mind," said Ha-Ya-To, shaking his head. "It was a bad joke . . . just like this whole day."

The two went to work, doing their best to ignore the thing they knew was up above, watching and waiting.

Ha-Ya-To was scanning his third computer bank when he found the data he was looking for. It was in code, but the Aero Booster's cockpit computer was able to crack it. He downloaded the file and pulled it up on his monitor screen. It was a report written by scientists who had been living in the Golden City long before the EXO-FORCE team had ever found the place. He began to read.

FILE: X1240974-1

PROJECT: Nightmare-3

GOAL: To create a weapon capable of defeating an invading force armed with battle machines.

SUMMARY: Projects Nightmare-1 and Nightmare-2 were abandoned when it was realized that any energy weapon capable of stopping a mass attack would require so much power, it would leave the Golden City defenseless after only one use. Project Nightmare-3 was then begun, with the goal of creating a *living* weapon for use against battle machines. After a number of failures, success has finally been achieved. In laboratory tests, the creature has shown the ability to destroy our most advanced battle machines in under five seconds.

Ha-Ya-To kept scanning. There was a diagram of the creature, which looked like a cross between a giant bat and a mythical dragon. Its claws and teeth were specially designed to tear through metal, even the ultra-hard zaylium armor that Golden City battle machines were made of. It was able to hide from human sight and all sensors, not showing any life signs unless it was on the move. Its skin was so tough and thick that it would take a massive energy blast to even slow it down. It was trained to spot battle machine movement and immediately attack. The creature could fly, see in the dark, and worse, it was smart — too smart.

FILE:	X1240974-1
FINAL REPORT:	This will be the last file recorded from this laboratory. Nightmare-3 has proved to be everything we hoped — and much more. It is too powerful. We cannot control it. All we can do is hope to contain it.

The report ended there. Ha-Ya-To could figure out the rest. The scientists fled, sealing the blast doors behind them and hoping that would keep the creature inside. It had — even this thing would have a problem with ten-foot-thick metal doors. Frustrated, the creature must have gone into some kind of hibernation. It stayed down here, waiting for someone to return to the lab and set it free, never realizing there was no one around to do it. The Golden City had been abandoned and everyone who knew of its existence was gone.

But the blast doors are open now — why hasn't it escaped already? Ha-Ya-To wondered. *Unless . . . it's never been outside the lab . . . it doesn't know there's a city up there. But if it finds out — and attacks — what will happen to EXO-FORCE?!*

The Aero Booster's alarms went off. The next second, metal beams torn from the ceiling were crashing into the row of computers. Sparks flew everywhere as the machines caught on fire. Ha-Ya-To looked up to see the creature in a power dive right for him.

A huge ball of flame erupted from the main computer bank. The creature screeched in anger and changed course, heading back up to its nest on the ceiling.

"The fire!" Ha-Ya-To shouted. "It doesn't like the fire!"

He used Aero Booster to pick up a burning beam and hurl it at the ceiling. The creature became visible just long enough to grab it out of the air. Ha-Ya-To waited for it to screech again or throw the beam away, but it did neither.

"The creature's actions disprove your theory about —" The robot's statement was cut off by both Aero Booster's and Shadow

Crawler's sensors sounding. The creature had decided to do something — something *very* bad. The burning beam was on its way back down with the speed of a missile, and it was headed right for the two battle machines!

CHAPTER 6

The metal beam hurled by the creature hit the Shadow Crawler dead-on, slamming into the battle machine's power cell. An electrical surge shot through the robot machine, sending it stumbling against the wall. Ha-Ya-To could see that the Devastator inside was feeling it, too, as the electric jolt scrambled its circuits.

I could just do nothing, Ha-Ya-To said to himself. *That would mean one less Shadow Crawler and one less robot to worry about.*

But even as the thought crossed his mind, Ha-Ya-To came to the Shadow Crawler's aid. Clamping a power cable onto the robot battle machine, Ha-Ya-To drew some of the electrical surge from the Shadow Crawler into Aero Booster. His battle machine converted it into energy, ending the danger to the robot.

When the crisis had passed, he removed the cable. The Shadow Crawler righted itself. The robot pilot stared at Ha-Ya-To. "Your actions were illogical. I am your enemy. Why did you act to continue my existence?"

Ha-Ya-To shrugged. "Because right now, we both have a bigger enemy than each other," he said.

"I will have to analyze," said the Devastator robot.

"Do it later," said Ha-Ya-To. He turned to see that the flames were dying down, extinguished by some automatic system built into the computers. "If fire doesn't bother that thing, what does?"

"The properties of fire are heat and light. Conclusion: The creature is vulnerable to —"

"Light," said Ha-Ya-To. "It sees in the dark, it lives in the dark . . . so its eyes are sensitive to bright light."

Ha-Ya-To thought fast. A powerful enough light might stop the creature long enough for him and the robot to make it out of the lab in one piece. But the lab lights were useless, and setting the rest of the place on fire probably wasn't a great idea. What other source of light could they use?

The answer hit Ha-Ya-To like a proton cannon burst. "Lasers! Lasers are light!"

"Neither Shadow Crawler nor Aero Booster can generate a laser of sufficient power to affect the creature for the required five-point-seven seconds needed to escape," said the Devastator.

"Remind me not to go to you when I need cheering up, tinhead," said Ha-Ya-To. "Well, if neither battle machine can do it alone, we'll do it together. We link machines for one big blast. If we hit it while it's close enough, we'll blind the thing long enough to get out of here."

Even as he said it, Ha-Ya-To knew how crazy it sounded. To link Shadow Crawler and Aero Booster together, both battle machines would have to power down. That meant he and the Devastator would have to trust each other. If one powered down and the other didn't, one battle machine would be vulnerable to a sneak attack.

To his surprise, the robot didn't protest. Instead, it said, "Commence system shutdown in five seconds. Five . . . four . . ."

Is it up to something? Ha-Ya-To thought. *Does it want me to shut off my machine so it can blast me, take the code, and try to get away?*

Ha-Ya-To shook his head. *No. If we are going to make it out of here, then I have to trust this pile of — this robot. There's no other choice.*

When the countdown hit one, Ha-Ya-To shut off all power to Aero Booster. The Shadow Crawler shut down at the same time.

Neither human nor robot said anything. They just opened the power core hatches on their battle machines and rapidly began connecting cables.

When they were finished, Shadow Crawler and Aero Booster were linked together by a tangled mass of wires. The idea was that the two machines could share power and fire a laser cannon burst twice as powerful and twice as bright as either could do alone. Of course, it was also possible that both battle machines might explode the second they were powered up, due to the sheer amount of energy they were channeling.

When Ha-Ya-To's machine came back online, his life sensors flashed again. The creature was on the move, circling overhead like a vulture, probably preparing to make another dive.

"Ready?" he asked.

"Yes," said the Devastator.

"Power up!"

Human and robot hands hit controls. Power surged through both battle machines, collecting into one massive pool of energy. Alarms went off inside both cockpits as pressure gauges surged into the red zone. Neither machine was built to contain this much raw power. It had to be released soon, or both battle machines would blow up.

The creature was still circling. *Come on, come on, dive!* thought Ha-Ya-To. *We need you at close range or this won't work!*

The smell of melted wiring filled the Aero Booster's cockpit. With nowhere to go, the energy was making a mess of the battle machine's inner workings.

It's attracted to battle machine movement, and ours can't move linked together like this, thought Ha-Ya-To. *But maybe there's something here that can.*

Ha-Ya-To climbed swiftly out of the cockpit of the Aero Booster and ran across the lab. He sought out the least damaged of the row of battle machines and got inside. His finger stabbed down on the controls, hoping that there was at least a couple of volts of power still in the machine.

The battered battle machine shuddered and bucked. Then suddenly lights were visible on the control board. It was powered up! The screens showed it had only enough power to take a few steps, but hopefully that would be enough. Ha-Ya-To triggered the movement control, and the battle machine started charging toward where Aero Booster and the Shadow Crawler stood.

The creature spotted the movement. It dove right for Ha-Ya-To's machine, moving impossibly fast. Ha-Ya-To dove out of the cockpit, hit the ground, rolled, and made it back to his feet. The creature was just reaching the abandoned battle machine, now just about out of power. The EXO-FORCE pilot leaped into the Aero Booster, shouting, "Now! Now!"

Ha-Ya-To and the Devastator hit their fire controls at the same split second. A massive laser blast shot from their linked machines, slamming into the creature. Even at this level of power, the blast couldn't pierce the creature's hide. But the laser's harsh glow was a devastating weapon. Temporarily blinded, the creature screeched and flapped its wings, trying to stay in the air.

At Ha-Ya-To's command, the arm of the Aero Booster slashed down, severing the connections with the Shadow Crawler. Both battle machines raced for the lab exit. Behind them, the creature's cries had changed from ones of pain to ones of rage.

Ha-Ya-To activated the Aero Booster's two remaining rocket engines as the Shadow Crawler rapidly scaled the wall of the shaft. Aero Booster quickly outdistanced the robot battle machine, reaching the surface first. Ha-Ya-To looked down to see the creature forcing its way through the lab door and into the shaft. All it would take would be one blast from his laser cannons to collapse the shaft, trapping both the creature and the Shadow Crawler below.

His weapon had enough energy and he had a wide-open shot. But for reasons even

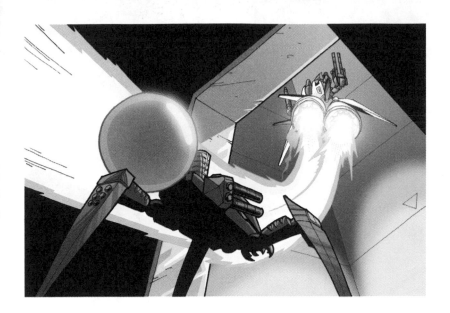

Ha-Ya-To would never be able to explain, he didn't fire. In a flash, the Shadow Crawler was out of the shaft and on solid ground. Both pilots fired their weapons, striking the ground and sending earth and rock raining down the shaft. An instant later, the miles-long tunnel caved in, burying the lab and the creature . . . perhaps forever.

Ha-Ya-To stared down at the pile of rock and dirt for a long time. "It's almost a shame," he said. "After all, what was that creature doing, other than its job? It just did it too well."

He looked up at the Devastator robot. "Now *we* have a job to get back to. Come on, then — attack. You're not getting this code."

The Devastator looked at Ha-Ya-To for a long time. Then it activated its communications device. "Devastator-37 reporting. Mission status . . . failure. Code is in a place where it cannot be accessed at this time. Returning to base."

Ha-Ya-To looked down. The magnetic code plate was still attached to Aero Booster. But the robot was saying it was someplace it couldn't be reached.

"Wait a second," he said. "Hold on. What you just reported in — I thought robots couldn't lie."

The Shadow Crawler turned and began to walk away. Then it stopped, turned, and faced Ha-Ya-To. "I am not lying, human," said the robot pilot. "At this moment, on this day, I cannot take the code from you. My behavior is illogical — I must evaluate. When I have done so, on some other day . . ."

No need to finish, thought Ha-Ya-To, watching the Shadow Crawler turn and head down the mountain. *On that other day, we'll be enemies blasting at each other again. We're both warriors — that's what we do. But maybe part of being a warrior is knowing when not to make war?*

Ha-Ya-To knew he should return the code to the Golden City right away. But instead, he triggered the Aero Booster's rocket pack and took off for the sky. He would fly for a long time, lost in thought, before bringing his battle machine home.